# COMPLICATED
# LOVE

# COMPLICATED LOVE

ALELOISE HARDY CROMARTIE,
LADY LOLO

XULON PRESS

Xulon Press
2301 Lucien Way #415
Maitland, FL 32751
407.339.4217
www.xulonpress.com

**xulon PRESS**

© 2023 by Aleloise Hardy Cromartie, Lady Lolo

Editors: Shinika Cromartie-Burth, Brenda Kitzmiller & Sheila Kesner
Illustrators: Kaliyah, Jasmine & Zaria Cromartie
Collaboratora and Cover Designer: Edoris Cromartie Jr.

All rights reserved solely by the author. The author guarantees all contents are original and do not infringe upon the legal rights of any other person or work. No part of this book may be reproduced in any form without the permission of the author.

Due to the changing nature of the Internet, if there are any web addresses, links, or URLs included in this manuscript, these may have been altered and may no longer be accessible. The views and opinions shared in this book belong solely to the author and do not necessarily reflect those of the publisher. The publisher therefore disclaims responsibility for the views or opinions expressed within the work.

Unless otherwise indicated, Scripture quotations taken from the King James Version (KJV) – *public domain*.

Scripture quotations taken from The Message (MSG). Copyright © 1993, 1994, 1995, 1996, 2000, 2001, 2002. Used by permission of NavPress Publishing Group. Used by permission. All rights reserved.

Paperback ISBN-13: 978-1-66286-914-3
Ebook ISBN-13: 978-1-66286-915-0

# DEDICATION

This novel is dedicated to the memory of my deceased son who passed away at the young age of 23 years old. His passion for life extends in the memories of family and friends to this very day. He was a loving child. No one had to wonder what he was thinking.

**His death gave birth to my passion for writing.**

Live on my son, you will always be cherished and remembered by all your family and friends.

EDORIS CROMARTIE III
SUNRISE: August 28, 1970
SUNSET: October 4, 1993

It started as a friendship then blossomed into so much more. Angel found herself torn between two lovers, finding it very hard to decide which one to let go. Angel, 20 years old and a gorgeous young lady, attends a satellite school of the University of New York where she is majoring in Creative Writing. She lives in a prestigious New York neighborhood where all the homes are assessed over two million dollars. Angel spends most of her time writing to avoid feeling bored and alone. A very talented young lady with the ability of grasping anything presented to her. Her only weakness, understanding the differences of a man's character. She lives with her only brother Victor who became her mentor and provider. Victor was thrust into a surrogate parenting position after the death of their parents 17 years earlier.

When Angel was twelve years old she experienced a medical condition that took her mind and body through a series of hospital and doctor visits. One morning she got up with one of the worst headaches she had ever experienced. Victor, with the advice of friends, doctored her with home remedies. After three days of being in continuous pain, Victor rushed Angel to the hospital. A CAT scan was done and to Victor's surprise, his sister had a deep Arteriovenous Malformation (AVM) Hemorrhage. The doctors explained to Victor the seriousness and informed him that she would have to be admitted into the hospital. The doctors also informed him that after the blood dissipated, Angel would need to see a Radiation Specialist. This is when Victor became the over protective brother. If he lost his sister forever it would be a devastating blow. Victor cancelled all of his appointments to stay by his sister's side. Two weeks later Angel was discharged. She began feeling like nothing had ever happened. A year later she underwent the one time radiation treatment and was told that there should not be a reoccurrence.

The worst of Angel's medical conditions were over. She began to live a normal life. She was a beautiful, vibrant, young lady. Her body was one of a desired model, 5'7" and 130 pounds. Wherever she went, all attention was on her.

Angel knew very little about the opposite sex. Her brother kept his sister very sheltered. While attending the University of New York satellite school, to avoid being alone Angel found a life on her own. Victor, an Architectural Engineer, begin to travel again wherever his job needed him to go, both national and international. Angel wanted for nothing except male companionship. She had very few female friends because of jealousy. She was exposed only to Victor's friends but under his watchful eyes because 99% of his friends were males.

One afternoon while leaving her creative writing class, she spotted a very attractive, tall, slim built, young man leaving the same building and walking to his car. Several weeks went by and it seemed as if Angel and this unknown young man left the building at the same time. Yet they never saw each other while in the two story building. "This is more than just a coincidence," Angel thought to herself.

She was not wrong. As Angel walked to her car one day she was suddenly approached by the young man.

"Excuse me but I've been noticing you for several weeks. Not to be presumptuous, but I know because I see you alone doesn't necessarily mean you don't have someone somewhere waiting for you. I can only speak for myself, and please forgive me, if you had any type of relationship with me, I would never let you leave this building unattended. Is there someone waiting for you?"

"What a come on line," Angel thought. "Victor didn't teach me this approach."

"I've been noticing you also and I've never seen anyone with you. I can ask you the same question." Angel said.

"No, I have no one waiting or anticipating my arrival," he said with a quick smile. "I have friends of the opposite sex but no committed relationship that would keep me from my next question. Will you allow me to treat you to dinner? I realize you don't know me so let me introduce myself, my name is Terrance. I am a 25 year old photography major with a studio located inside this building. I also collaborate with writers because sometimes photographic illustrations are needed. You can tell me where you would like to go. Since we are just being verbally introduced, you may not feel comfortable with me coming to pick you up from your home. Tell me the place, the time and I'll meet you there."

"That sounds great. If you know where Mario's restaurant is we can meet there at 7."

She purposely didn't tell him the location of the restaurant for a reason. If he truly was a resident of this city he would automatically know.

"Mario's restaurant at 7, confirmation noted. I'm sorry but I became so excited to finally get the courage to approach you, I forgot to ask your name." He said.

"My name is Angel," she said with a childish smile.

As she went to open her car door, his hands made it to the handle first.

"Thank you," she said. "I'll meet you at the restaurant. Try not to be late."

"You are welcome and believe me I will be on time. See you later Miss Angel."

Angel went home, took a bath then proceeded to get dressed for dinner with Terrance. In her mind she remembered the old saying you can't judge a book by its cover, but with him he really seemed to be a respectable and responsible guy. Victor always preached to her to never go out without letting him know where she was going and with who she would be with. She called Victor.

"This is Victor, I am in a meeting please leave a message."

"Hi Victor, I'm going to meet a young man I met for dinner. We've been seeing each other from a distance for several weeks, and today he decided to approach me. His name is Terrance, and he has a studio in the building downtown where my creative writing class is held. I'll tell you more when we speak, call when you can."

She did what her brother asked so now to Mario's for dinner with Terrance. Terrance got to the restaurant early and was outside waiting for Angel. As soon as he saw her drive into the parking lot he ran to greet her.

"I told you I wouldn't be late." Terrance took Angel by the hand to lead her into the restaurant.

They ate dinner and got better acquainted with each other. Terrance now knew the room where Angel's class was held. Angel found out where Terrance's studio was located. To both of their surprise, the rooms were several doors from each other. At the end of the meal Terrance walked Angel to her car and they both said good night. This was the beginning of a 'NO MORE NIGHTS ALONE' writing her inward feelings through poetry.

*Complicated Love*

Angel found someone she could go out with and have a great time; Laugh, dance, be merry, and forget all that troubled her mind. Terrance and Angel began to see each other frequently, three to four times weekly. They went out to eat, went shopping, went to movie theatres, dances, and take long walks in the park. It appeared to be ideal in the beginning, but for some reason something was missing. Angel felt a lack of genuine connection. Yes, she began to have feelings for Terrance, but the type of connection she always dreamed of was not present. After all the good times with this young man when she found herself alone, she was lonely.

Angel was home alone when the telephone rang. "Hello this is Angel may I help you?"

"Yes you may my dear, you miss your brother?"

'You know I do Victor. When are you coming home?"

"It looks like I'll be in California several more weeks. I need a huge favor."

"What my beloved brother, your wish is my command."

"First how was dinner with Terrance? Did he treat you well? Can't wait to meet him to lay down the golden rules."

"Slow down, he's a good person. I have tons of fun with him just no real connection. He does anything to make me happy but, I don't know," she sighed. "What is it you need me to do?"

"My suit designer, Eric, just called to tell me my clothes are ready for pick up. You think Terrance would mind taking you?"

"Anything I ask him he'll do. I'll call him. How do I get to Eric?"

"I'll text you his address and number."

Angel completed the call with Victor and immediately called Terrance's office.

"May I speak with Terrance please, this is Angel."

"Hold on I'll see if he can take your call," the secretary replied.

"Angel my love what do I owe the honor of your call?"

"Sorry to interfere during your working hours. Victor called and needs me to pick up his clothing from his tailor. I can drive but it's located in the hectic part of town. Do you think you would be able to take me later today or tomorrow, at your convenience, of course?"

"Business is slow today, what time will you be ready?"

"Its 1:00 now, will 2:00 be okay?"

"Yes, I'll be there soon."

Angel got ready and waited for Terrance. To insure the shop would be open she called Eric to verify what Victor had told her.

"Good afternoon, this is Eric's Tailoring, how may I assist you."

"Good afternoon may I speak with Eric? This is Victor's sister Angel."

"What a pleasant surprise, this is Eric. Victor told me to expect a call from you."

"I just needed to make sure that his suits were ready for pick up. I should be there in about an hour if that's all right?"

"That would be perfectly fine. However, I told Victor I would deliver them to your house. You don't have to come way out here and try to find parking plus traffic is very hectic today, I'll be glad to deliver them to you."

"Victor never told me you would deliver, just wait until I talk to him. Any way I called a friend, and it's too late to cancel. I'll see you soon."

"If you insist, looking forward to finally getting a chance to meet you. Victor has talked a lot about you. See you soon, drive safely."

"Why didn't Victor allow his tailor to bring the suits here," Angel wondered.

*Complicated Love*

Angel decided to call Victor for an answer.

"Hello Angel you got the suits already?"

"No Victor, I'm calling to ask why you wouldn't allow Eric to deliver them to the house. He told me you knew he would."

"First of all, I don't trust Eric alone with you. He is something else," Victor said with a chuckle in his voice.

"It makes no sense Victor. You trust me with Terrance, someone you don't know; but you won't trust Eric, someone you supposedly know. Or truth be told, is it that you don't trust me. I'm confused."

"Confused or not you'll understand when you meet him. Promise you won't be taken in by his charms."

"My curiosity is really at an elevated level. Is he committed to anyone?" Angel asked her brother.

"No, but he is genuinely looking. Why?"

"Just asking Victor. I'll call you later the doorbell is ringing, it must be Terrance."

"Who is it?" Angel asked before opening the door.

"It's me babe. Open the door."

The minute Angel opened the door Terrance did something he hadn't done in the months they've been seeing each other and going out. He put his arms around her, looked into her eyes, lifted her off her feet and kissed her passionately.

"I refuse to wait any longer to say this, I LOVE YOU ANGEL."

Breathless, unable to utter a word, she took him by his hand and finally was able to say, "Let's go before the store close."

The look on Terrance face was one of shock and surprise. Angel gave no response to the kiss or to what Terrance had just said. All she could do was rush to his car. He made it to the car just in time to open the door for her. Angel got in, her mind randomly wondering what to say. "Terrance, what just happened? Where did that come from?"

"My heart baby, my heart. Unfortunately for me it seems as if the feelings are only in my heart. Are you angry at me?"

"No, just stunned. Let's get Victor's suits then we will go someplace quiet to talk. Thanks for taking the time from your busy day to do this. I truly appreciate it."

"You're welcome. I'm glad you called me. What's the address?"

*Complicated Love*

Angel gave the address to Terrance. When they got to the store Eric was standing at the entrance. Before Terrance could completely park Eric was approaching the vehicle.

"You must be Victor's sister, Angel," Eric exclaimed as he opened the car door.

Terrance and Angel looked in Eric's direction strangely.

"Yes, I'm Angel how did you know?"

"Victor talked about you so much I asked to see a picture of you. The picture does you no justice. You are as beautiful as your name. Please forgive my forwardness."

Terrance, being the man he really is, approached Eric and in a stern voice said, "Excuse me, do I know you?"

"I'm sorry, didn't mean to disrespect you."

Eric turned and went back into the store. Terrance starred at Angel and in a perplexed voice said, "I'm truly glad I came with you. I don't know if you can trust this guy."

"He's been Victor's tailor for years. He knows better," Angel said jokingly.

To Terrance it was not a joking moment. He wondered how Angel could take Eric's actions so calmly. In his mind he really began to wonder if this was actually the first time the two met or was he the one getting played.

Angel visualized why Victor never invited her to go with him for a fitting. She also understood why her brother didn't have Eric deliver the suits to her. Eric, from his initial appearance, seemed to be a ladies man. He was about 6'4", 290 pounds, all muscle and no younger than 32 years old. No wonder Victor never introduced Eric to his sister. There may have been an immediate attraction and with that in mind, Victor was not going to take a chance. Eric was a great tailor, and Victor was not ready to search out another one. The safest thing to do was to KEEP EVERYTHING BUSINESS AND NOT LET IT GET PERSONAL. Eric was not a bad person with a flawed character. In fact he was a very business minded, serious person. In Victor's eyes, no one was good enough for his sister even though he knew, in reality, that someday she would meet someone to start a life of her own.

Terrance and Angel went inside, got Victor's suits and left. No words were spoken until Terrance got Angel home. He got out, opened her car door, and walked her to the front door of her house. He checked to make sure everything was safe, looked at Angel and said, "Make sure you lock the door. Call me if you need anything else." Terrance turned and walked away.

"Terrance, what did I do? Why are you so upset? Don't leave like this! Come inside, please."

"Are you sure? The way you were acting with Victor's tailor, I could have sworn the two of you knew each other."

"Terrence, you're jealous," Angel said smiling. "Come here."

As Terrance started walking up the steps to the house Angel ran down, grabbed him then planted a big kiss on his lips.

"My baby has a jealous side to his personality. I'll make you a delicious meal that should make you feel better. The old cliché says a way to a man's heart is through his stomach. Let's see if that's true."

"I can tell you now food may be one of the ways but if given a choice, all I need is you," Terrance said in a sexy voice.

Terrance followed Angel in the house with his arms around her waist.

"Wait a minute, you got me so off track your brother's suits are still in the car."

They both began to laugh hysterically as Terrance went back to his car to get the suits.

"I'm going to start cooking," Angel yelled.

Angel proceeded to the kitchen. She was so happy in her spirit she began to sing the song "IF YOU DON'T KNOW ME BY NOW, YOU WILL NEVER EVER KNOW ME."

Was the connection missing finally beginning to surface? Terrance got the suits. As he entered the house he heard Angel singing. All his frustrations quickly disappeared.

"An earthly Angel with an angelic voice. Be nice, remember I am a man with masculine emotions. It's not good to fool with Mother Nature," Terrance uttered softly.

"Where do you want me to put the suits?"

"When you get to the top of the stairs, the second door on your right. Please hang them in the closet."

"Yes ma'am, your wish is my command and never doubt or forget that."

"Just take them upstairs then come to eat," Angel said smiling.

Terrance did as he was told. He put the suits away, skipped downstairs in a jovial manner, went into the kitchen, and washed his hands. "So what are we eating?"

"Food", she said jokingly. "Just sit down and enjoy."

The entire time they were eating neither of them could resist playing footsie. They continuously touched each other's shoes under the table.

"The meal was delicious. I hate to eat and run but believe me it's the smartest thing to do. Before I go let me help you clean the kitchen. Maybe tomorrow after we've both cooled down, if you're amenable to me taking you dancing, I'll come to get you at 7 PM."

*Complicated Love*

"Sounds like a solid plan. You don't have to help me. Just leave! It will give me something to do in order to keep my mind occupied. Thank you again and I'll see you tomorrow at 7."

"Are you sure, I don't mind helping. It's not fair for you to cook, clean and be in this house alone."

"Enough," Angel said. "Please go. Let's not make this any more complicated than it is."

Terrance walked over to Angel and just held her body tightly against his. No words were spoken, just a body language which meant it's really time to leave.

"See you tomorrow. Are you sure you don't need me to stay the night. I will sleep downstairs. Hate leaving you alone," Terrance said as he was being escorted to the front door.

"I will be fine. It's not the first night alone, and it definitely won't be the last one. If I need you I will call."

"Good night, I'll check on you later."

Terrance left. Angel cleaned the kitchen then proceeded upstairs to get dressed for another night with no one to verbally communicate with. At least she thought.

Before she could get up the steps the telephone rang, it was Victor.

"Angel my beloved how are you?"

"Absolutely great my brother. Terrance took me to get your suits, even though they could have been delivered here," Angel said chuckling. "They are beautiful suits. Terrance put them in your closet."

"Wait a minute, Terrance went upstairs?"

"Calm down. He only did what I instructed him to do. You didn't think I would leave them on the couch until you arrived did you? That's ok don't answer that."

"Where is Terrance now?"

"On his way home I guess, Victor."

"Great! I'll be home in two days. I called Eric. He couldn't stop telling me how nasty I've been not allowing the two of you to meet. He asked my permission to come visit you in hopes you would allow him to take you out. I informed him that he would have to wait until I get home."

"Brother, do I have a 'SAY SO' in my life?"

"Glad you asked, NO! See you in two days. If you need anything call me and I'll get someone to you immediately. Good night precious sister."

"Good night over protective brother. I've got to get you someone other than your job to take up your time," Angel said laughing.

"Sleep tight Angel, see you soon."

Angel proceeded up the stairs again. She took a hot bath, looked for a good movie to watch and just as she was about to get in bed her cell rang. It was Terrance.

"Just calling like I promised. What are you doing?"

"I just took a bath and was about to get in bed to watch a movie."

"I've got to talk to Victor, this makes no sense."

"What doesn't make sense Terrance?"

"You in that huge house alone. Especially when I could have been there with you."

Before Angel could respond, a call from a number she didn't recognize came through on her cell. She wondered who was calling. Normally she wouldn't answer calls from an unknown number especially if she was alone. This time was different.

"Terrance hold on, don't hang up."

"Yes can I help you?"

"I'm glad you answered, this is Eric."

"Oh my goodness," Angel thought.

"It was still early, I wanted to apologize for this afternoon. Do you have a few minutes to talk?"

"Yes, hold on a second." Angel placed Eric on hold.

"Terrance, thanks for holding, it was Victor checking on me. I'm exhausted, see you tomorrow."

She lied.

"Sleep well, good night." Terrance hung up thinking Angel was about to go to sleep.

She hesitated then clicked over to the other line.

"Eric, Victor's suits were picked up so why are you calling?"

"To apologize for not respecting the man you came with. I should have never approached either of you the way I did. Victor failed to mention you were dating someone."

"It's not me you owe the apology. You should be apologizing to my friend. We go out together to have fun but I'm not intimate with him."

"I will," Eric said to her. "Give me his name and number."

At that moment Angel caught herself, "Why am I explaining myself to this man. He just met me today. Let me put a stop to his madness," she thought.

"Eric, no apology necessary, goodnight." Angel immediately hung up the phone.

Months went by, Angel and Terrance continued going out on dates to the movies, the malls, shopping and dinner at various locations.

Eric wouldn't take no for an answer from Victor when trying to get permission to see Angel. He took it upon himself to periodically call Angel to check on her. Strangely Angel began to look forward to hearing Eric's voice on the other end of the line. She began to feel the type of connection with Eric she was looking to have with Terrance. Complicated situation arising to say the least. Victor finally gave his permission for Eric and Angel to see each other. Months and months passed. Angel staggered between the two male companionships. Finally she became tired of the game. Innocent or not, she was tired and was forced into making a choice.

Eric was quite unique and different for with him she could be herself. If she felt like crying Eric was there to comfort and console her. If she needed someone to be serious with, Eric was there with a listening ear. She loved them dearly but for different reasons. Now the crossroad was near. She loved them both but was IN LOVE with only one. She could no longer juggle between the two. It had become a heavy burden. A decision had to be made quickly. So what's true love got to do with it, *EVERYTHING,* now that she has to let one go.

When alone at night she tossed and turned. Peaceful rest was not an option. Would a bond of friendship be possible remembering the intimacy they once shared? Terrance fulfilled her fun side while Eric had etched his presence in her heart. She told herself every day would never always be a fun day. However, every day she'd have choices to make.

"I need to choose the one who will be my soul mate. The one who will always treat me as his Queen. I need to choose the one I can be vulnerable with knowing he will never take advantage of my feelings or break my heart."

"I've got to be careful how I tell the one I'll be leaving, I'll be going on into the future with another. I will not play with the one I'm leaving emotions, because I wouldn't want him to do that to me. I know... I'll start by not going out as much. I'll cut back slowly on our visits. I'll become very cordial and timid with him and hope he'll get the picture and just walk away."

Angel keep referring to the future with or without HIM. Who is the HIM?

"How did I let myself get caught up in this situation? They both completed a missing part of my life. I promise to never put that burden on anyone else. It is my responsibility to do whatever it takes to complete myself."

To rest her brain she started on a writing assignment for her class.

*Complicated Love*

HAVE YOU EVER THOUGHT DEEPLY ABOUT THE WORDS TO THIS PARTICULAR LOVE SONG? DID THE SONGWRITER WRITE IT LITERALLY OR FIGURATIVELY? YOU BE THE JUDGE!!!

<u>IF YOU CAN'T BE WITH THE ONE YOU LOVE, LOVE THE ONE YOU'RE WITH</u>

MY INTERPRETATION, LOVE YOURSELF.

THINK ABOUT IT. IF YOU CAN'T BE WITH THE ONE YOU LOVE,
**ANOTHER BEING,**
WHO ELSE IS LEFT...**YOU!**

SO LOVE THE ONE YOU'RE WITH
DOES NOT NECESSARILY MEAN ANOTHER PERSON. YOU ARE WITH YOURSELF 24/7, 365 AND EVERY FOUR YEARS 366 DAYS.

SO REMEMBER,
IF YOU CAN'T BE WITH THE ONE YOU LOVE,
LOVE THE ONE YOU ARE ALWAYS WITH,
**YOURSELF.**

"Eric and Terrance have traits I have grown to love and respect. There's nothing I can really do or say at this stage that will spare the one I leave from heartache and pain." Angel rehearsed her justification in her head. She finally got the nerves to make her first call.

*Complicated Love*

"Hi Terrance, can we meet this afternoon at Mario's for lunch? I have something we must discuss."

"Yes, why meet there I'll come get you. Are you ok you sound as if you've been crying?"

"I'm fine just got a lot on my mind. It's ok I'll meet you at Mario's at 3."

"Ok my love I'll see you there. I love you!" Terrance hung up the phone.

Anticipating what she was about to do, emotions began to emerge. Angel fell to the floor sobbing. She didn't want to hurt Terrance but there was no way not to. She knew who she wanted to be with and unfortunate for Terrance, he would not be the one chosen. While on the floor crying her bedroom door opened.

"Baby why are you crying? Did you hurt yourself, tell me what's wrong!" Eric ran and sat on the floor with Angel. As Eric held her she buried her head into his chest. The tears rolled uncontrollably.

"Angel, baby, please tell me why are you so upset? I can't stand to see you cry. Let me help you."

Angel couldn't stop crying so Eric picked her up, took her into the bathroom, and began to put cold water on her face. She looked up into his beautiful, genuinely caring eyes. After calming down she walked slowly from her bathroom into her bedroom. In a soft voice she said "I need to tell you something, and I pray you will understand."

"You can tell me anything, what's wrong?"

She looked at her watch, it was almost one o'clock.

"I need you to sit down; please don't draw any conclusions until I'm through talking, PLEASE! I never stopped going out with Terrance," Angel timidly said.

Eric not knowing what to say or what to do looked at Angel with tears in his eyes. "What did you say?"

"Come here, sit beside me."

Eric walked slowly toward Angel keeping eye-to-eye contact with her.

"I told you after we really got to know each other that I was going to end it with Terrance as my boyfriend. I didn't. Remember the day you saw Terrance walking in the mall with me holding hands, and I told you it was just a friendly gesture. The time you came over and I was on the telephone laughing uncontrollably, it was with Terrance. The night I went out and you tried to call me and got no answer, I was with Terrance. Eric I never meant for this to happen. I never intended to hurt you. I just found it hard, at that time, to hurt Terrance. However, now I know who it is I really want and need."

Eric stood up, dropped his head while fighting back anguish and tears screamed out "Angel, why? Where did I go wrong? What is it you needed that I failed to see? I've got to go!"

"Wait!" Angel said in a louder voice. "Baby please let me finish. I love you in a way I could never love Terrance."

At that point Eric couldn't stand to be in the same room with her. He looked at her with hurt, pain, disgust and disappointment plastered on his face. He walked over, kissed her, and swiftly exited her room.

Time was approaching to meet Terrance. Angel ran to the top of the stairs outside her room just to watch her true love, leave her house hurt and confused with no idea that he was the one she chose to live her life with. Not having a lot of time to ponder her future plans with Eric, Angel went to her room to get dressed to confront Terrance.

Angel arrived at Mario's at 2:30. To her surprise, Terrance was already there. When he saw her he ran and greeted her with the warmest embrace.

"I thought you'd never get here," Terrance whispered softly in Angel's ear.

"Let's hope you feel the same about me after I tell you really what I have to say."

"This seems serious, maybe we shouldn't go inside. Let's go to my car instead," Terrance responded.

"Where is your car?" Angel asked him while wondering if she should go to his car or tell him really why she wanted to meet him in a public setting. Reminiscing over Eric's reactions, would Terrance be any different? Not sure, just knowing he would never physically do any harm to her, she decided to have the conversation in his car.

He placed his arms around Angel's waist as they walked to his car. He politely opened the car door for her then proceeded to the driver's side. He got in and looked sternly at Angel as she glazed out the front window. Solemn minutes seemed like hours. Terrance looking at her, Angel looking straight ahead, trying to get in her head the exact words to say before letting it come from her mouth.

Terrance reached over, grabbed Angel's hand, turned her face to him and said,

"Okay, let's have it! What's going on inside that beautiful head of yours?"

"I can't continue to see you." she whispered in a low voice.

"I'm sorry there must be something wrong with my ears. What was it I know I didn't hear you say?"

"Terrance, I just can't do this anymore."

"Can't do what Angel," Terrance responded with an elevated voice.

Just that fast the man with the calm spirit now irate.

"I've been dating you and Eric. You fulfilled the fun side of my life. Eric fulfilled the needed to be understood part of my life. I am not proud of my actions. The truth is I am very ashamed for not being truthful to either of you."

Terrance could no longer hide his feelings. In his face one could sense anger, disgust and genuine pain. He looked away, as if in a trance, tears began to run down his cheeks. Slowly he turned toward Angel. "I refuse to accept what you just said, so tell me the truth. Are you telling me after all these years our relationship was a joke? Nothing we did, nothing we shared meant anything but a good time with each other? No Angel, you may try to believe that lie but I know better. You wanted to meet me today to tell me we are through? You could have told me that on the telephone. Is it that you had to see the reaction on my face? Get out of my car right now! I need time to think."

To Angel's surprise, Terrance reached across her body, opened her door and without having to say another word, Angel knew he meant just what he said,

"GET OUT." She touched his hand and said "Please let's not end this way."

How was the man expected to act after being told years later the woman he thought he was seeing exclusively had been splitting her time with another man?

Terrance didn't have to say another word, his stare was soul cutting. Angel knew at that point to be quiet and exit the car which she hesitantly did.

Without another word being uttered, Terrance speedily drove away without closing the passenger door.

Angel, sobbing uncontrollably, began to walk to her car crossing lanes of traffic without looking. One car just barely missed her. She never noticed how close she was to being hit. She made it to her car and realized she had left her purse in Terrance's vehicle. Fortunately she had placed her cell in her pants pocket so she immediately gave Terrance a call.

"What now?" he answered and said. "You forgot to hurt me more! I started not to answer. What do you want Angel? I've got places to go, people to console."

"I left my purse with my keys inside your car. It's getting dark and it looks as if it's about to rain."

"Well I guess you need to start walking and find a place to stay dry."

"Terrance, please! I realize you are upset right now but I know you didn't mean what you just said."

There was complete silence on the phone because Terrance disconnected the call.

Angel dialed his cell again, no answer.

"I know he sees that it's me calling. What am I going to do?"

Angel leaned on her car and began crying and talking out loud. "I will step on my pride and call Eric." Eric's telephone went straight to voicemail. That has never happened to her prior to their last conversation.

"Wow, the two men who meant the world to me lost in one day! I should have kept my feelings to myself. Now look at me, I'm cold, I'm hungry, and it's about to rain. If I call my brother, all hell will break loose. I just won't allow that to happen."

At this point, Angel became out of control. She began to run around her car, hitting, with her hands, the trunk, the hood, the windows, taking out frustrations on an innocent vehicle. It was at this time a young man saw what she was doing, pulled his car behind Angel's and said, "Young lady, what's wrong? Did someone rob you, have you been assaulted? Why are you so upset? Give me your keys. I'll sit with you in your car until you calm down. Let me help you!"

He grabbed Angel's hands before she could land another blow to her vehicle.

"I don't have my keys, they are with someone else. It's about to rain…"

The stranger stopped her.

"Is that why you are so upset? It will be all right. I know you don't know me, my name is Anthony Santiago. I'm an attorney. You can call my office to verify. Please get into my car, and I'll take you wherever you want to go. Just stop crying, relax, you will be fine, I'll make sure of that."

Angel looked at him, eyes red from crying, "You'll take me wherever I want to go?"

"Yes."

"Take me to 42$^{nd}$ Street and Pines Drive."

"Wait a minute, it's almost 7 PM, and you want me to drop you there? Are you crazy or just ready to be humiliated, tortured and raped? No, before I do that, I'll pretend as if I never talked to you, call the police and report a crazy woman in need of help. Now where is it you want me to take you?"

"To be truthful, I really don't care. I just know I can't go home. I just lost two of my best friends in one day, hours apart and it was all my fault."

"I'm so sorry, how did they die?"

*Complicated Love*

Angel looked into the stranger eyes, started laughing and sarcastically said, "They're not physically dead. I told my two lovers about each other. You figure out what happened. You did say you are an attorney, right?"

Stunned at the response, he took Angel by her hand to lead her to his car. He called his office to inform his secretary that he would be taking the rest of the day off and to reschedule all his appointments. "Tell them I had an unexpected family emergency."

Angel looked at Anthony. "Who is this man?" she wondered. "He doesn't know anything about my situation, or me, yet he's cancelling appointments to make sure I'm safe. This is surreal."

"Where are we going?" Angel asked.

"You specifically told me that you didn't want to go home so I'm taking you to eat, and then I'm taking you to my place. First, I'm going to go shopping. You look as if you're a size 12, am I right?"

"Yes, but shopping for what?"

"You are a beautiful person who is in need of a change of clothing. When I walk into the restaurant with you, I want you to feel comfortable and right now you wouldn't be. If you would rather not go out, I will make dinner for you. Just tell me what you would prefer. Just don't ask me to drop you off on 42$^{nd}$ Street. Beautiful lady which do you prefer, go shopping then out to eat or my place? Your desire will be honored and totally respected."

"Take me to your place, please!"

As Anthony proceeded driving to his place, Angel starred at him. "Who is this stranger? What does he really want? Am I safe or should I really be afraid? Even with the uncertainties, I don't want to go home. I pray I'm not making the dumbest mistake of my life."

"Anthony, I left my purse in the last male friend's car and I have no money. I don't even have any identification to get money from my bank when it opens. My car keys are also in my purse."

"First of all you are with me and will need no money. However, you do need your purse for your keys. Where does he live? I'll get your purse. As far as the car is concerned, with your permission, I'll call a friend of mine who owns a towing company to have your car towed to my place or yours. I can have a locksmith come and cut you a new set of keys. Princess, what do you want me to do?"

Anthony looked at Angel with such a comforting smile.

"I will not have you go get my purse. Call your friend and have him tow to your place. Thank you, I'll find a way to repay your kindness and generosity I promise."

*Complicated Love*

"The only repayment I need, even though we just met, is for you to trust me, put a smile on that pretty face of yours and know I got you and from this point on, you'll never cry or want for anything. As the songwriter wrote in his lyrics, LEAN ON ME BABY. Forgive me for calling you baby this early in our meeting. I realize it has only been a few minutes I've known you but it feels as if I've known you forever. I've never had any court case I could not find an argument for until now. Strange as it may seem, I can't stop or factually argue how you are making, without trying, my heart react to your presence. I almost feel as if I am in the twilight zone."

Angel is bewildered. "There is no way a man of this character is without someone special in his life. He's an attorney, a very handsome man, polite, gentle and not committed to another person. At least I'm assuming he's not in a committed relationship. How could he if he's taking me to his place unannounced? Not to a hotel but to his place."

"Anthony, wait, please pull over, I must ask you something and don't lie, please tell me the truth. Won't your lady get angry with you for bringing a stranger home?"

Anthony pulled over looked at Angel and began to laugh.

"What's so funny? Why are you laughing?"

"I feel better now. I was wondering how long it would take the woman in you to come out to ask me that question. There is no other lady anymore. Like you, I was in love. My ex decided my work hours were too long and I had contact with too many other women. I swear I never cheated on her nor did I ever get close to. Not believing me, she took up with another man and left. I got home to find a note on the kitchen counter saying the wedding is cancelled, I'm gone."

"I am so sorry. How long were you in the relationship?"

"I invested four years, 3 months, five days, ten hours, 38 minutes, 49 seconds, but who's counting?"

"I understand. I juggled between two men for two years and in one day, destroyed it all when I decided to confess and tell the truth."

"You are not telling me that one of the guys left you knowing you could not get into your vehicle? In plain words, left you helpless after all those years! Please tell me how to get to his house, his apartment. I want to confront him."

"No, this is not your battle. I created this monster and someway I'll settle it."

"How can you be so compassionate? Suppose someone, other than myself had stopped, saw your state of mind and took advantage of you? No, unforgiveable. He could have at least made sure you got in your car and was safe. Past years meant nothing to him? How could anyone get that angry and leave someone who they say they loved or had strong feelings in a vulnerable state of mind? I can't, nor will I try to understand how he could do that. In fact I won't stand hearing you defend the creep."

"Who have I lucked up on? Slow down, it hasn't been 24 hours. Don't allow vulnerability cloud who you really are." Angel thought.

Anthony drove into the driveway of a luxurious house. It reminded Angel of her home.

"This is beautiful. You live here alone?"

"Yes unfortunately. I work all week and most weekends. I pick up something on the way in to eat. As a matter of fact the kitchen has never been used."

"Do you have any groceries in the house?"

"No, never had a reason to buy groceries. I'm only home long enough to bathe and sleep."

"This weekend you do. Let's not get out. If you don't mind I saw a mall a few blocks away. We can get something for me to cook. If I can borrow a little cash I need to get a few personal things. I promise to pay you back."

"First of all, no you can't borrow any money. I will take you to the clothing store and get anything you want or need."

"Anthony forgive me, in the midst of everything I forgot about the jewelry I'm wearing. It's worth a lot of money.

*Complicated Love*

Maybe there's a pawn shop in the mall. I will get cash that way."

"Don't' let me began to think you only have a pretty face and no brains. I told you I've got this and you."

"Ok, I introduced myself and foolishly never got your name. What is your name angel face?"

"Angel," she said with a childish giggle.

"Are you for real? An angel face whose name is Angel, now I know I am not just lucky but also a highly favored man. Please don't take this as a move on you, but lean over here and let me kiss your forehead."

She complied with the request and Anthony kissed her gently on her forehead.

"Now, I'm taking you shopping Miss Angel."

"Thank you my knight in shining armor."

Smiling, beginning to think everything was going to turn out favorably, Anthony took Angel shopping. Instead of going to the mall closest to his home, he took Angel to the largest mall in town. In fact Angel had shopped there many times. It was one of the places she and Terrance visited quite often.

"Come on my Angel, let's go shopping. Get whatever your heart desire on me."

He went around the car, opened the door, took Angel by her hand and said,

"Which store first?"

In one store while Angel was trying on clothing, Anthony told her to take her time he needed to do something but promised to be right back. Three hours later they left the mall with four bags. Three belonging to Angel. A smaller bag had some things Anthony purchased for Angel as a surprise.

They arrived at Anthony's house, gathered their bags and went inside.

"It is really beautiful in here Anthony. Who is your decorator?"

"Why, do you need something decorated?"

"Yes I do."

"How soon would you like to meet the person responsible for what you say you like?"

"How soon can you get the appointment?"

"Would right now be a good time?"

"You've got to be joking. How can it be now and I'm here with you?"

"My beautiful, innocent nature Angel, you are talking with the decorator."

"No way you did all of this!"

"I see I have a lot of convincing to do. Let me show you where to change."

Anthony showed Angel a room with a Jacuzzi style tub and an enormous shower. He placed the bags on the bed and started walking toward the bedroom door. "Take your time call me if you need me. I won't shut the door completely so that I will be able to hear you."

He looked at Angel from the doorway and blew a kiss her way.

Angel took the things Anthony bought her out of the bags. She heard a light knock on her door.

"Are you still dressed?"

"Yes, come in."

"I'm sorry I forgot to do something. May I?"

"Yes, I am a guest in your house."

"Once you entered with me you are no longer a guest. I give you the same rights that I have."

Angel, for the first time in her life, was speechless.

*Complicated Love*

Anthony had a bottle of something in his hand. Angel tried to see what it was but couldn't. He went into the bathroom, started the water in the Jacuzzi and squeezed something from the bottle he had in his hand.

"What are you doing?" She asked.

He turned around smiling and replied, "You've had an exhausting day. I forgot to turn the Jacuzzi on for you. I also put lavender in your water to help you relax."

"Wow!" What a thoughtful man. The female who left him had to be crazy. I thought I was in love, NOT!"

"Let me know when you're out of the Jacuzzi, presentable, and I'll massage your legs. Stop your brain, an innocent massage. Not your body, just your legs. You have been on them a long time today."

"You won't just be massaging my legs. Unknowingly to you, it will be my mind." Angel said to herself.

The warm pulsating water with the fragrance of lavender was just what the doctor ordered. Anthony sat patiently in his living room anxiously anticipating Angel to summon him. After what seemed to be hours, Anthony went to the bedroom door, "Angel, are you alright?"

"Yes, I'll be out soon. I didn't realize how exhausted I really was until you provided me with a piece of heavenly rest."

*Complicated Love*

"No rush. Just checking to make sure you didn't fall asleep. Call me whenever you get out."

Anthony realized he didn't get anything for them to cook. Not knowing what his new friend liked, he decided to order for delivery, three different pizzas, a variety of Chinese food and lasagna with garlic rolls.

Angel decided not to inform Anthony that she was out of the Jacuzzi. In her state of mind she thought, why gamble with her feelings which were already out of control. Mentally she said to herself "I am not going to allow this relationship to start off wrong. I am going to see what God has in store for us. I failed to consult him with Terrance and Eric. This time I won't."

Angel began to pray.

"Heavenly Father forgive me for all the things I've done wrong. Let your unconditional love, mercy and grace be with me always. In the midst of weakness, I ask for your strength. And since you know the end at the beginning of everything, don't allow me to do anything that will displease you tonight. Amen."

Angel put lotion all over her body and sprayed lightly the perfume Anthony bought for her. Looking through the clothes purchased, she put on a very conservative pair of pants with a low cut matching blouse. She took a deep breath, walked slowly to the bedroom door, opened it and said, "Thank you again for your hospitality,"

"Wow, what a transformation. You are gorgeous. Why didn't you call me?"

"We just met this afternoon. Neither one of us really know anything about each other. I definitely didn't want you to think of me as a lady with little or no values. Most importantly, I didn't want our emotions to cloud all that has happened today and get the best of us. Neither one of us can afford to play with fire. There's something special and different about you I have never experienced in my entire life. I've been in two relationships I just knew were leading to an everlasting life with one of them. Never have I felt what I feel with you. I will not allow a lack of judgement to taint this, NO WAY."

Touching her hair so gently he said, "You are so right. What would have started out so very innocently could have and probably would have, gotten out of control. You have had such a traumatic day. I just wanted to soothe some of the pains to make you feel relaxed and comfortable. Thank you for doing what my mind would have said was right, but in the end which would have won? My mind or my body? I am a man."

"I can't and won't argue against that. A man you truly are," Angel softly said.

Anthony showed Angel around his house. As they were about to sit on the couch, the doorbell rang.

"Anthony, are you expecting someone? You need me to go into the bedroom?"

He looked at her and smiled, "No, it's our dinner. Not knowing what you liked I took it upon myself to order a variety of foods."

Anthony opened the door, paid for the food which arrived at the same time, looked at Angel and said, "What will it be, Chinese, Italian or Pizza?"

"God where has this man been all my life. Don't let me say or do anything that will make him have second thoughts, please. It's written in your Word that faith is the substance of things hoped for evidence not seen. I need your direction and guidance." Angel whispered.

"Earth to Angel, which do you prefer?" Anthony said in a joking voice.

"I am so sorry, whatever you eat I'll eat. You haven't advised me incorrectly thus far and I doubt if you will now."

"Chinese cuisine my love?"

"Yes, did you order sweet and sour chicken?"

Anthony began laughing hysterically. "Amazing. Yes I ordered it because it is one of my favorite dishes."

"Thank you God for sending me my Angel," Anthony thought gazing toward the heavens.

The two ate, laughed about silly things and as all good things evidentially come to an end, the question was asked by Anthony, "So what do we do now. You can sleep in the guest room, or I can take you home."

Before Angel could answer her cell rang, it was Eric.

"Aren't you going to answer?" Anthony asked.

"No."

Her cell rang again, this time it was Terrance.

"Before you ask, no I refuse to talk to either of them."

Looking at the message indicator blinking, Anthony got up and began to walk away.

"Where are you going?" Angel asked.

"I see they left you messages. Call me after you listen to them, and I'll take you home if that's what you want to do."

"Don't leave, I want you here with me while I see what the two of them has to say. Come on, sit by me, please."

Anthony obliged her and sat next to Angel.

"Angel, Eric, I am sorry for exiting the way I did. I let my emotions control my heart. I need to see you, please call me. If I don't hear from you soon, I'll take it upon myself to knock on your front door. I can't let it end this way. I love you." Angel looked at Anthony, tears in her eyes. Anthony put his arms around Angel and said, "It's okay, play the next message, you can do this. I'm not going to let you handle this alone. Always know I got you."

"Angel, it's me Terrance. Emotions should have never made me leave you vulnerable to danger. I've been calling your house so many times that your brother is questioning me about your whereabouts. Angel, where are you? Please call me. I was wrong I need to talk to you!"

Angel's cell rings again, it was Eric. Before that call ended, Terrance was calling again.

"Angel, call your brother or let me call him to let him know you are perfectly fine and that I'll be bringing you home," Anthony suggested.

It wasn't five seconds after Anthony told Angel to call her brother, Victor was calling her.

"Hello Victor what's wrong?"

"What is going on? Eric and Terrance are calling the house back to back. I asked them where is my sister and neither one could tell me. I waited patiently for as long as I could, are you okay and where are you?"

"Victor, I am better than okay."

Anthony beckoned to Angel to allow him to speak to Victor. She immediately, without any hesitation, passed the cell to Anthony.

"Hello Victor my name is Anthony. I can assure you, your sister is perfectly safe, and I'll be bringing her home as soon as she's through eating dinner."

"Anthony who? I've never heard about you. Who are you, where do you live? You don't have to bring her I'll come and get her. What is your address?"

Hearing Victor's frustration Angel tapped Anthony's hand, "Let me talk to him."

"Victor, I'll answer any and all questions you have for me but right now your sister would like to speak with you." Anthony passed the cell to Angel.

"Victor, please calm down. I will explain everything as soon as I get home. I am safe, in great hands and will be there soon. I love you, goodbye."

Not another word was said. Angel disconnected the call and fell into the arms of her Knight in Shining Armor, Anthony. The tears flowed, the sobs grew louder. Anthony pulled Angel closer to him and held her so lovingly tight.

"Get it all out baby. I got you."

Several minutes later they both looked at each other and agreed that they were no longer hungry.

"Come on, get your things, I'm taking you home even though I really don't want to. We'll have dinner another time. Unless Divine intervention says otherwise, this is only the beginning, I promise you."

Angel and Anthony gathered her belongings from the bedroom and walked silently to his car.

"What is your address my lovely lady?"

Anthony didn't want to add to Angel's demeanor by having her direct him to where she lived. He programmed the address into his navigator and commenced to driving his new friend home.

Angel called Victor, "I'm on the way. If either one of those jerks call you, please do not tell them you talked to me and definitely don't let them know I'm on my way home."

"Anything you say. How far away are you?"

"I should be there in about thirty minutes. Love you brother."

Angel reached across the console, grabbed Anthony's hand, pulled it to her chest and softly kissed it.

"There's no way anyone would believe we just met and the attraction would be this strong. I can't begin to tell you how blessed I am that God sent YOU to my rescue. You think you can find it in your heart to call me occasionally?"

"You didn't hear a thing I've been saying to you. Wait a minute as soon as I park I want to say what I have to say holding you near my heart. Why? So, that you can feel my heart beating next to yours."

He pulled into Angel's driveway, got out, opened her door and did just what he said. Anthony placed Angel's head on his chest so that she could feel the beating of his heart. He squeezed her tightly yet gentle and said, "Feel that heartbeat? It now belongs to two. Our God and you; now and forever. This is the first day of the rest of our lives, living separately, but in spirit, together. That is, once you get your head clear, if you really want me. The decision is all yours to make. The short time we've been together without any doubt or hesitation in my mind, I know we can build a great relationship. I also realize that everything I feel in my heart happened unexpectedly and so very sudden. How can this be? I assured myself, after my last breakup, that I would be surrounded with so much work a social life would be the farthest from my mind. I don't want to rush anything, nor will I pressure you. When I leave your home today, it will be so hard. I'll wait to hear from you. Hoping and praying to see and talk to you again."

The front door of her house opened, it was Victor running out to greet Anthony and to check to make sure his one and only sister was indeed okay.

"Angel, I am so glad you are here and safe."

Victor looked toward Anthony, "Come in I need to talk to you."

They all went into the house, Victor with his arms around his sister's waist.

"Victor, I am Anthony Santiago. I am a lawyer and a partner of a prestigious local firm. I have been an attorney for 10 years, never married and no children. I saw your sister in need of help."

Angel interrupted, "Victor, if Anthony hadn't stopped I honestly don't know if I would standing here right now. This man is not the one you should be drilling."

"Angel," Anthony said, "It will be okay. Your brother is doing no more than I would be doing if the shoe was on the other foot."

"Victor, have you eaten?" Angel asked her brother.

"No, why?"

"I am starving and I know Anthony is also."

"I thought you were having dinner when I called."

"There were so many distractions we lost our appetite. You two continue your conversation while I make us something to eat."

Anthony looked at Angel, "That's not necessary. You are tired and exhausted. I saw many restaurants on the way here. We can all go out, talk over dinner, or I'll get what you want and bring it back. You do not have to cook tonight."

Victor stared at Anthony with admiration. "He may not be so bad after all," he thought to himself. "I've always said first impressions tell a person's true nature. I don't know the entire story. After being around Terrance for months and already knowing Eric, I could not get completely comfortable with either of them. If they left my sister in a vulnerable situation, I can now understand why."

Looking at Victor and Anthony, Angel smiled and walked toward the kitchen.

"Anthony," Victor said, "that's the look of I heard what you said, but I'm not listening to the words you said."

Victor and Anthony smiled as they walked to the living room to continue their conversation.

Angel was in another world. The day that started off as one from a horror movie has now become a modern day Cinderella adventure. Her thoughts and feelings for Eric and Terrance are slowly becoming a figment of her imagination. She wondered how that could be so easy to do when she truly thought her feelings for Eric would lead to something more serious. Until that morning, Eric was the one she had decided to spend the rest of her life with. Has that feeling really changed? Just as she was about to mentally create a meal to remember, the silhouette of Eric was standing at the kitchen door. She went to make sure Victor and Anthony were still getting to know each other, slightly closed the entrance door to the kitchen, and swiftly proceeded to the back door.

"Why are you here? I don't remember telling you to come over and most importantly why are you in my backyard staring at me through my kitchen door? Eric, you stormed out of here this morning, now you've decided to come back, unannounced. Are you drunk or crazy?"

Angel felt weird talking to Eric so irately. How would she have felt? How would she have handled it if it was Eric explaining having an affair with another woman? Questions she could not avoid seeking the answers.

"Forgive me, I'm sorry, I had a horrible misjudgment in my actions. To answer your questions, no I'm not crazy and you know I don't drink. I miss my best friend and lover. I came to the back of your house to sit by the pool. I was searching for the right words to say to you. I heard commotion in the kitchen and to my surprise, it was you. Angel, please allow me to come in? I should have buried my hurt pride, discussed rationally with you exactly what happened and why. I need to apologize to Victor. I have called him so many times trying to get in contact with you. I must let him know I was wrong."

In an angry unsympathetic voice, "What you can do for me and I highly suggest you do, is to leave now on your own or I'll have my brother do it for you. Don't let it get worse than it already is. I'm not saying we won't talk I just can't do it this minute."

"Call him. I'm not leaving until we talk. No that's alright. I know what I have to do."

Without saying another word, Eric left. At least that's what Angel thought. "It's not meant for any of us to eat tonight. I give up! I'll tell the men no dinner. I'm going to bed."

Angel started out of the kitchen and to her surprise, the doorbell rang. "Victor, it's Eric, I must speak with you in person."

Angel ran to the door, however, not fast enough. When Victor and Anthony heard the doorbell and Eric's voice, they both rushed to let him in. As Victor opened the door Angel grabbed Anthony by his arm, led him into the living room and said, "I need you to leave; I promise I'll call you later. Thank you for getting me home safely."

Anthony kissed Angel on her forehead, walked past Eric and Victor and said, "Have a great evening."

"Thank you for bringing my sister home, we'll talk."

Eric's facial expression showed a frown that spoke words without him opening his mouth. In his mind he thought, "Who the heck is this man Victor is thanking for bringing my girl home safe. When and why was she ever in danger?"

Anthony exited without looking back. Silence covered the room as Victor, Angel and Eric stood motionless. Several minutes passed, "Angel you and Eric get it together. If you need me I'll be upstairs."

There was a large sectional in the Foyer area of the house. Angel immediately went to the farthest side away from Eric. She sat with her back to Eric.

"Angel, who was that man? Why was Victor thanking him for getting you home safely? When I left you were safe."

Walking briskly toward Angel, "Talk to me."

"Why? You stormed out before I could tell you I decided not to straddle the fence anymore. I was about to tell you how much I loved you and wanted your forgiveness. I was crazy enough to think you would understand, forgive me and allow me to stay in your life. I was so wrong."

Angel's cell rang, "Hello Terrance, I need my purse."

"That's why I'm calling. I'm on my way to drop it off at your house. We must talk. I am so sorry for my actions today. I can understand you not wanting to see me or talk to me right now. I accept the responsibility of being totally wrong for what I said and most importantly for not making sure you got into your car. I know you don't want to see me, so I'll leave it in the chair on the back porch. Take care and when things calm down we must talk."

*Complicated Love*

Before Angel could tell him she was home, Terrance ended the call.

Angel's mind began to soar. "Wow, what a jerk. Sad to say since I spent so much time with him I now see I was a bigger jerk. How could I have read him so wrong? He left me on the side of the street, unable to get into my car and all he has to say is I just wanted you to know I'm leaving your purse on your back porch. Not once did he ask are you alright. Do you need me to come get you? Where are you?"

Angel, with tears again streaming down her face, sat on the couch curled in a ball, suddenly felt a pair of arms around her. She found herself being comforted twice in one day by two different men. Some women have gone a lifetime and have never been held affectionately by one.

Stop your mind, she is not promiscuous, just a person with COMPLICATED LOVE issues. In a state of hurt and confusion it is very easy for one to allow emotions to become tainted. Reality and fantasy, whose meanings are so different, began to seem like one and the same. Angel always knew Eric was more of the family type; however, for two years she allowed Terrance to share the fun part of her life she thought would be missing in Eric.

"I'm not going to ask what that call was about. When you are ready to let me know, I'll be here. Allow me to say this. I heard what Terrance said. When he gets here, you stay where you are, I'll get your purse. Listen to me carefully, YOU WILL NOT SEE OR TALK TO HIM ANYMORE

TODAY. I sincerely hope he delivers your purse like he said he would, get back in his car and leave."

Eric tilted Angel's head to the side and with his hands began to wipe her tears away.

"Eric, I am so sorry. After you left so abruptly without giving me a chance to tell you it was you I wanted, I went berserk. I..."

Eric stopped her, "Not now my love, later. I need you to go upstairs, wash your face and as soon as I get your purse I'll come up. Will you do that for me?"

As a child looks into their parents face with sorrowful eyes, she smiled and said, "That I can do."

Angel got up with a burst of revitalized energy and ran upstairs to wash her face. In the midst of washing her face she saw her reflection in the mirror and thought to herself, "Enough is enough. You've let your emotions get the best of you now snap out of it and be the woman you know you are. No more tears today."

Angel washed her face and began to sing, "Mercy said NO!" Her spirit was renewed. Angel had an assignment due for class so she decided to write a poem to herself and to any one in need of encouragement or direction on how to face compromising circumstances and/or situations.

*Complicated Love*

WHAT IS IT LIKE TO LOVE SOMEONE AND FEEL AS IF
YOU'RE IN IT ALL ALONE.
YOU THOUGHT YOU HAD FOUND A KNIGHT IN
SHINING ARMOR,
BUT TO HIM YOU'RE JUST ANOTHER FEMALE
HE HAS CONQUERED AND LEFT HURT AND SCORNED.

WOMEN HAVE GOT TO LEARN TO BE PATIENT.
DON'T FORCE YOUR FEELINGS ON SOMEONE WHO HAS
NOT GROWN.
BE AROUND HIM, STUDY HIM AND WATCH HIS
ACTIONS CLOSELY.
THEY WILL SELDOM STEER YOU WRONG.

NEVER THINK YOU CAN CHANGE SOMEONE,
ONLY GOD HAS THE POWER TO DO THAT.
GOD STILL GIVES A PERSON FREE WILL,
ALLOWING THAT INDIVIDUAL THE DECISION,
TO DO RIGHT OR WRONG.

SO WHO ARE WE AS A MORTAL BEING
TO THINK WE HAVE MORE AUTHORITY THAN GOD.
A PERSON MAY CAMOUFLAGE CHANGE TO
ACCOMMODATE THE SITUATION; AND WITHOUT ANY
FIGHT OR NEW REVELATION,
REVERT BACK TO THEIR COMFORT ZONE.
BE VERY WATCHFUL OF HIS ACTIONS,
DOES HE TRY TOO HARD TO SHOW A SIDE THAT'S
REALLY NOT HIM? IS HE COMFORTABLE, RELAXED
AND POISED,
IF CONFRONTED WHEN HE'S ALL ALONE?

LISTEN TO THE WORDS THAT COMES OUT OF
HIS MOUTH.
IT'S MAY SOUND CUTE TO SAY "I LOVE YOU TO DEATH."
WHY NOT NURTURE THIS SAYING,
"I LOVE YOU TO LIFE AND ON THAT YOU CAN
ALWAYS DEPEND."

LOOK AT HOW HE TREATS HIS MOTHER AND THE
OTHER WOMEN IN HIS LIFE.
YOU BETTER BELIEVE IF IT'S NEGATIVE, YOU WILL BE
THAT RECIPIENT IN YOUR FUTURE LIFE.

DON'T RUSH TO LOSE YOUR FREEDOM AND
INDEPENDENCE,
THINKING YOU WILL ALWAYS FEEL THE SPARKS YOU
MAY BE EXPERIENCING NOW. YOU BETTER MAKE SURE
THERE IS A SOLID FOUNDATION,
IF YOU PLAN TO LIVE BLISSFULLY A HAPPY LIFE.

"Eric no need to come up I'm perfectly fine. I'll be down soon," Angel yelled to Eric.

Eric didn't hear Angel because he was about to exit the house to confront Terrance who was there to leave Angel's purse on the back porch.

"What a cowardly gesture," Eric said to Terrance. "I have no idea what really happened today and frankly I don't give a ....."

"Excuse you! Since you're here take, Angel's purse and get out of my space," exclaimed Terrance in an agitated voice.

*Complicated Love*

Eric grabbed Angel's purse from Terrance.

"Terrance only you, Angel and some stranger by the name of Anthony really know what took place today. Humor me and complete the missing parts of this puzzle. I know for a fact when I left her this morning, I was upset, she was upset but safe in her home. Humor me, what transpired?"

Terrance gazed at Eric, clutched his fists, walked past Eric turned and said in a mediocre voice,

"Let your woman tell you. Her name is no longer Angel in my vocabulary."

As swiftly as Terrance appeared, he disappeared even faster.

It's now very late. Eric wanted to give Angel her purse then leave but somewhere he found compassion and remembered hearing she had not eaten all day. Eric never had to cook. Someone always prepared meals for him. Tonight would be an exception. Eric went into the kitchen, looked inside the pantry and refrigerator to see what he could prepare expeditiously. In twenty minutes Eric walked to Angel's room, knocked on the door, "Is it alright to come in I have two things to give you?"

"Sure, come in."

"Here's your purse and I made something for you to eat."

*Complicated Love*

Stunned because to give her the purse Eric had to encounter seeing Terrance. What superseded her finally receiving her purse was the fact Eric had prepared food.

"Eric, we'll talk about how you got the purse later. You made me something to eat? You shouldn't have but since you did, thank you."

Eric smiled, reached out took Angel by her arm and escorted her to a chair located in the corner of her room.

"Sit down my Princess. I am sorry I left the way I did today without giving you a chance to say all you had to say. My punishment for that, will be issued to me by me. Open your mouth and let me feed you my beloved. I was about to leave but my conscience wouldn't let me because I knew you hadn't eaten all day. I hope you enjoy the bacon, egg and cheese toast sandwich I have for you. So open your mouth and eat."

Like a child whose parent was instructing what they wanted their child to do, Angel's eyes swelled with tears again, something she said she was through doing, as she sensuously opened her mouth to consume the sandwich Eric had made for her.

"Um, this is really tasty and to think you made this all by yourself. When did you become a chef?"

They both began to laugh.

"Let's not get carried away. Are you laughing with me or at me?" Eric responded as he continued to feed Angel the sandwich.

The sandwich was consumed, Eric wiped Angel's mouth. He passed her the drink she already had in her room, kissed her on the forehead and said, "Goodnight my love, get some rest I'll see you in the morning."

"Don't leave I need to talk to you."

"Not tonight I promise we will tomorrow."

Eric left the room quickly because he knew if Angel insisted again, he wouldn't have the strength to walk away.

Eric's feelings for Angel were more intense than he really wanted to believe. Being told that she was involved with another man, on the human side got the best of him. He had to have time to clear his head to be able to act from his heart. Questions clouded his mind as to how he could have been so blind.

Eric and Anthony repeatedly tried to contact Angel. Each time they called her house telephone or cell, she refused to answer. On different occasions they tried knocking on her door, she still refused to answer. Anthony became very worried and decided to send a letter to Angel. Eric called Victor.

"Hello this is Victor how can I help you?"

"Victor, Eric, how is Angel? I've been calling but for some reason she won't answer. I went to your house unannounced, and before you say anything I apologize, I need to see her. Can you or should I say will you make that happen?"

"First of all thanks for inquiring about my sister. To answer your question regarding her well- being, she's fine. She has decided to devote her mind and time to her studies. She's scheduled to graduate in three months."

"That's it?" Eric responded with delight.

"What is it Eric?"

"We can plan a gigantic graduation party. Don't worry I'll take care of all the details."

"Eric, take a deep breath and breathe. I'll call you when I get home this weekend."

"I hear you but in the meantime when you see me I'll have an itinerary ready to be implemented."

Victor laughed, "See you soon Eric, goodbye."

So much has happened in Angel's life until she almost forgot to register for the final semester of her creative writing class. She had to make the decision if she wanted to continue going to class and risk the chance of running into Terrance or register for an online course. After looking at her syllabus she found she could do both.

Without hesitation she put her personal feelings aside in order to complete her education.

"If I indulge myself with class work, I won't have time to ponder on what's going on in my life," she thought to herself.

The first few weeks Angel's online courses were just what the doctor ordered. Then boredom set in. Since Victor was always traveling Angel begin to feel enslaved. Online classes with no socialization became unbearable. She had not opened the letter she had received from Anthony. "What harm will it do to read it," she thought.

> "DEAREST AND MOST BELOVED ANGEL, WHY HAVE YOU MADE IT IMPOSSIBLE FOR ME TO TALK WITH YOU? THE LAST FEW MONTHS HAVE BEEN MISERABLE. I WAS ONCE THE BEST ATTORNEY, ALWAYS ON TOP OF MY GAME. NOW, I SPEND COUNTLESS HOURS THINKING OF YOU. I DRIVE BY YOUR HOUSE EVERY SINGLE DAY HOPING TO SEE YOU. BABY, DON'T SHUT ME OUT. THE SHORT TIME GOD ALLOWED YOU AND ME TO BE TOGETHER SHOULD NOT BE TAKEN FOR GRANITE. I'VE INSTRUCTED BY SECRETARY TO INFORM ME OF A CALL FROM YOU EVEN IF I'M DOING A CLOSING CASE ARGUMENT. THAT'S HOW SERIOUS I AM ABOUT PRESERVING MY RELATIONSHIP WITH YOU. PLEASE FIND IT IN YOUR HEART TO CALL ME. MISSING YOU DRASTICALLY!" ANTHONY.

"I can't do this anymore. If I don't make a change I'll really lose my mind. I know what I'll do, I'm going to take two days of online courses and physically attend classes for two days. I only have a few months to go. What's the worst thing that can happen? Finally have a confrontation with Terrance?"

Every day for weeks Angel would rush into her classroom and look carefully outside trying to make sure Terrance was not present. She would rush to her car and quickly leave the campus. Confrontation with Terrance was inevitable. One afternoon before she could reach her car she felt the presence of the man she had not seen or spoken to for months, Terrance. He was standing three cars away from where she had parked. When Terrance saw that she was close to the vehicle, nervously, he approached her.

"Don't panic, I'm not going to harm you. I need to apologize. I noticed your car the first day you came back. I just got up enough nerves to approach you. I can't blame you if you never forgive me, I just pray somewhere in your heart you will. I take full responsibility for my actions.

Angel I am a different man. I can't tell you how many times I picked up the telephone but because of my embarrassment never completed the call. I have driven by your house every day since I foolishly did what I did. I've asked God to forgive me, now again I'm pleading to you for forgiveness."

Angel is in total shock. Terrance in an open parking lot was on his knees, crying and begging for Angel to forgive

*Complicated Love*

him. He was not pretending, Terrance was coming from his heart.

"Get up Terrance! You're making a spectacle of yourself. People will think you are mad."

"I don't care. I was mad when I left you the way I did. It hurts me to think about that afternoon. Eric would have been justified in his actions the night I dropped your purse off to your house. I was a fool!" Terrance sobbing more.

"I can't do this now Terrance," Angel said. "Get up, go back to your office. I've got to go. I have a lot of assignments to complete."

Angel got in her car and left. Terrance, wiping his face, got up just to watch Angel drive away.

"God I need your Divine intervention," Terrance said looking toward heaven with his hands extended. "I love her!"

As Angel drove home her eyes swelled with tears visualizing Terrance begging her to forgive him. She immediately dismissed what had just happened. There was no time for her personal life; she had too many assignments to complete.

Angel's assignments were easy ones. She had to write a variety of poems: BALLAD (a poem which tells a story); BIO (a poem about one's life, personality traits, ambitions);

*Complicated Love*

EPIC(an extensive serious poem); FREE VERSE(a poem written in rhymed or unrhymed lines); LYRIC(a poem that expresses thoughts and feelings); NAME(poetry that tells about a word); ODE(a poem that is serious or meditative in nature); and ROMANTICISM(a poem about nature and love having emphasis on a personal experience). Angel began to let her mind wonder.

*************

SMILE When your heart is shaking.
SMILE Even though you're faking.
SMILE When your eyes are full and surprised.
SMILE Even though you're worried,
       Know that God is always there for you.
SMILE Through all your trials and troubles,
       Knowing that God will never leave or deceive you.

*************

Many things may come against you,
from the ones you least expect.
You'll sometimes feel discouraged, never give up or give in.
Trials come to test you so you can see who you really are.
Give them all to Jesus, let Him your burden barrier be.

*************

*Complicated Love*

**ALONE** IN A CROWDED ROOM,
HOW CAN THAT POSSIBLY BE?
PEOPLE STANDING ALL AROUND ME,
SMILING, LAUGHING AND DOING THEIR OWN THING.

WHAT HAVE I DONE TO DESERVE THIS?
WHAT HAVE I ALLOWED TO TAKE PLACE?
NO MATTER HOW LARGE THE CROWD IS,
I STAND ALONE IN A LONELY SPACE.

I'M NOT A BAD OR EVIL PERSON.
I GET ALONG QUITE WELL WITH FAMILY AND FRIENDS.
I JUST FIND IT HARD TO ENJOY PEOPLE IN
CROWDED PLACES,
WITH DECEIPTFUL SMILES PERTRUDING FROM
THEIR FACE.

*************

**DADDY'S** LITTLE GIRL

I remember the first time I saw your little face.
I knew then and there it was from God's amazing grace.
So innocent, so pure, a definite gift from above.
My baby, my heartbeat, DADDY'S LITTLE GIRL.

You are maturing so quickly, but one thing you can
be assured,
No matter how old you become,
YOU'LL ALWAYS BE DADDY'S LITTLE GIRL.

The distance between us will mean nothing at all.

*Complicated Love*

If you need me, just call me, I'll never let you fall.
Remember I love you and that will always be.
You're daddy's baby; you're daddy's heartbeat,
YOU'LL ALWAYS BE, DADDY'S LITTLE GIRL.

*************

**Children** are blessings from Heaven,
Loaned to us from God above.
We are to nurture, teach and guide them,
According to God's holy and righteous plan.

Teach them patience and unselfishness,
And that we are not here to live alone.
We must show them how to share with others,
As God shared with us His only son.

*************

**GOD'S** GIFT TO MAN WAS WHEN HE GAVE, HIS ONLY BEGOTTEN SON.
HE GAVE HIS **SON** TO GIVE US **SUN** WHENEVER DARK CLOUDS WOULD ARISE.
UNCONDITIONAL LOVE, UNDESCRIBABLE PEACE, ETERNAL LIFE WE WOULD ALWAYS HAVE,
IF ONLY WE ACCEPT HIS GIFT, AND LIVE BY HIS HOLY PLAN.

GOD'S GIFT TO MAN IS GIVEN TO ANYONE WHO ACCEPTS JESUS CHRIST AS THEIR KING.
TREATING EVERY MAN AS THEIR BROTHER, RESISTING EVIL FORCING IT TO FLEE.

*Complicated Love*

GOD'S GIFT GIVES US MERCY ADORNED WITH BEAUTY
AND GRACE.
HIS GIFT LETS US KNOW WE CAN MAKE IT, NO MATTER
HOW LONG IT TAKES.

HE WILL CARRY ON HIS SHOULDERS ALL OUR BURDENS
AND OUR WOES.
THROUGH THE WILDERNESS HE WILL GUIDE US,
UNTIL WE FIND SAFETY IN A PEACEFUL PLACE.

************

**WHILE** RIDING IN AN AIRCRAFT MADE BY
MAN'S OWN HAND.
I CAME IN TOUCH WITH JESUS AND HIS GLORY
FROM ABOVE.
HIS GREATNESS AND HIS MAJESTY PERMEATED
THROUGH THE CLOUDS.
ONE MUST REALLY BE AN ATHEIST TO SAY AND THINK
THERE IS NO GOD.

I TOLD MY GUARDIAN ANGEL TO GUIDE ME THROUGH
THE CLOUDS.
TO SAFELY TAKE ME TO MY LOVED ONES, WHO WAITED
FOR ME ON THE GROUND.

WHILE LOOKING OUT THE PLANE'S WINDOW, ONTO
THE CLOUDS BELOW.
I COULD ONLY WONDER WHY SOME PEOPLE
AROUND ME,
COULD BE ENGULFED WITH THE LIQUOR THEY CHOSE.

*Complicated Love*

I SEE GOD'S BEAUTY IN EVERYTHING, WHILE RIDING IN THE AIR.
I FEEL HIS PRESENCE NEAR ME, AND KNOW HOW MUCH HE CARES.

*************

WHEN WE KNEW NOTHING ABOUT EACH OTHER,
THE CHEMISTRY SEEMED TO BE SO STRONG.
AS WE GOT CLOSER AND LIVED TOGETHER,
THE FLAWS IN OUR CHARACTER WERE NOT SO SWEET.

WE PROMISED TO LOVE AND RESPECT EACH OTHER,
NO MATTER HOW ROUGH THE SEA.
EVERYDAY WAS NOT PROMISED TO BE SUNNY,
MANY THORNS WOULD BE UNDER OUR FEET.

LET US REMEMBER HOW WE FELT IN THE BEGINNING;
LET NOTHING DAMPER OUR WAY.
LET'S CONTINUE TO SEE THE LIGHT AT THE END OF THE TUNNEL,
AND KEEP PRESSING FORWARD FERVERENTLY.

WE MUST BE VIGILANT ON HOW WE TALK AND TREAT EACH OTHER.
ONCE WE'VE SPOKEN THE WORDS WE CAN'T RESCIND.
IT'S NOT WHAT GOES IN THAT DEFILES A RELATIONSHIP,
IT'S WHAT COMES OUT BECAUSE THAT'S STRAIGHT FROM THE HEART.
LOVE CAN BE COMPARED TO WINE,
AS IT AGES IT GETS BETTER WITH TIME.

*Complicated Love*

ARE WE NOT BETTER THAN A BOTTLE OF AGED WINE?
CAN'T WE ALSO GET BETTER WITH TIME?

*************

MY DARLING, DARLING DAUGHTER, I LOVE YOU
OH SO MUCH.
I WISH THAT I COULD SHIELD AND PROTECT YOU,
BUT GOD SAID I'VE DONE ENOUGH.

I'VE TAUGHT YOU HOW TO LOVE HIM, AND ASK HIM
WHAT IS HIS WILL?
TO UNDERSTAND LIFES EXPERIENCES, AND MOVE ON
WITH THE GUST TO LIVE.

I'VE TAUGHT YOU HOW GOD LOVES YOU AND TOLD
YOU HE'D NEVER LEAVE YOU.
I'VE TAUGHT YOU OF HIS MERCY, AND HOW IS GRACE
WILL SEE YOU THROUGH.

HE GAVE YOU A GREAT FAMILY WHO TESTS YOU
CONSTANTLY.
ONE DAY THEY'LL BE YOUR HELPERS AND LIKE ME
YOU'LL SEE THEM GROW.

NURTURE THEM WITH KINDNESS AND PAMPER THEM
WITH LOVE.
NEVER, EVER GET DISGUSTED AND SAY YOU CAN'T
WAIT UNTIL THEY GO.

SOME DAYS MAY SEEM REAL LONELY, EVEN WHEN
YOUR HOME IS FULL.

## JUST REMEMBER GOD IS ALWAYS WITH YOU, AND WILL NEVER LET YOU GO.

Final assignments were completed and submitted. Angel was never concerned about her final grades. It would have surprised her if she got less than an A. She was now ready to start planning the next phase of her life.

The day of Angel's graduation had finally come. Her instructor praised the exemplary work she had submitted. Victor was excited for his sister but uncertainties were settling in for now he knew she wanted to travel.

"Good morning sunshine," Victor said to his sister as he stood in his sister's bedroom door. "Are you excited about today?"

"Good morning my beloved brother, yes I am. What's exciting me more is trying to find out what you've planned for me after the graduation ceremonies. Can the graduate get a little clue?"

"No," Victor said with a smile, kissed his sister on her forehead and walked away. "I'll be waiting for you downstairs."

While Angel was getting dressed, her cell began ringing. She looked at the caller ID, it was Anthony. She wanted to answer, however, she decided it would be to her advantage not to. She got dressed, left her cell on her bed, and rushed downstairs to Victor for her commencement.

Ceremony time had finally arrived. There were 200 young men and women in cap and gown anxiously waiting for the processional. The music began with each graduate marching from behind a curtain to their assigned seats.

The Dean of the school went through the preliminaries then announced the speaker for the occasion.

"This afternoon's speaker is someone who graduated from our school several years ago. He is now a prominent figure in our community. He is here to let you know when life gives you lemons, don't fold, don't give in, STAY ON FAITH STREET, and make lemonade. I am so proud to introduce to you our dynamic speaker, Anthony Santiago."

"What? Is that why he was calling," Angel could not believe what was happening.

> "Good evening to all in attendance today. It is an honor to stand before you and address this graduating class. When the Dean called to ask if I would I be available, without any hesitancy, you can tell my response. I accepted for two reasons: The first, was to encourage the young people you see before you today to never give up. Always strive to do your best. You speak to any circumstance or situation, don't allow it to speak to you.
>
> The second reason, there's a young lady in this class who has inspired me to take a genuine look at myself. I am here today because of her.

The speech went on for several minutes with the crowd searching for the identity of the young woman. Any smart person could have easily figured out who the mystery woman was if they had payed attention to Angel's face. Victor starred at his sister and smiled.

"Victor knew Anthony was the speaker and didn't tell me, WOW," Angel thought to herself.

> In closing, pursue your dreams with passion. Be careful of the people you include into your inner circle. Trust your instincts, it has been placed there by God.
>
> Thank you and God's blessings be with you. Confront your Future in confidence knowing NO WEAPON FORMED AGAINST YOU SHALL PROSPER (Psalm 91). If He takes you to it, He will get you through it.

The graduation celebration was a success. Angel had no idea that Victor wasn't the sponsor. Just before its conclusion, Victor had another surprise.

"Angel, I am so proud of your accomplishments. However, before we conclude this joyous occasion I have a challenge to present to you."

"What now?" Angel thought smiling at her brother.

"Five young men, chosen randomly, would like to give some encouraging words. Are you up for the challenge?" Victor said looking at his sister.

"Yes, let the challenge begin."

Victor began to explain the challenge.

"The challenge has rules. First, you will have a blindfold placed over your eyes. Secondly, you must listen carefully to each young man. You will two minutes to decide which young man impressed you the most by writing or scribbling the number of the voice which impressed you the most. The one chosen will have $25,000.00 donated to the charity of institution of their choice. Finally, you must go out on a one night's date. These young men have been screened for your safety. Are you ready?"

"My brother, my brother, you are truly a work in progress," Angel exclaimed. "Yes, I'm ready."

A blindfold was placed over Angel's eyes. She was given a pen and a sheet of paper in order to blindly write down her choice. Unknowingly to Angel, the young men voices would be distorted. In order for it to be truly an honest choice, the men could not speak of anything that would give Angel a clue to their identity. A Biblical verse or saying had to be quoted. The following is the order in which they spoke:

     1st Anthony
     2nd A stranger

*Complicated Love*

3rd Eric
4th A stranger
5th Terrance

Victor had to tell Terrance, Eric and Anthony that today had nothing to do with what had previously transpired between them. Today was all about his sister. The three agreed to put their differences aside and began to search for a scripture that would describe who they were in hopes they would be the one chosen by the woman they all deeply admired and loved.

The challenge for Angel's heart began.

Anthony   Corinthians 12:4-8
           Love is patient and kind; loves does not envy or boast; it is not arrogant or rude. It does not insist on its own way.

Stanger    Psalm 121
           I will lift up mine eyes unto the hills from whence cometh my help.

Eric       1 Corinthians 13:13
           And now these three remain: faith, hope and love.
           But the greatest of these is love.

Stranger   Romans 12:9
           Love must be sincere. Hate what is evil; cling to what is good.

*Complicated Love*

Terrance    1 Peter 4:8
            Above all, love each other deeply; because loves covers a multitude of sins.

"Well done," Victor said to the participants. "The decision now lies in the hand of my sister."

Angel, please remove the blindfold and inform us of your decision. Your date is anxiously awaiting."

Angel's mind began strategically pondering on why her brother would present her with such a challenge. He knew the status of her relationships because each of the men in her life found a way to convey to him what was happening.

"I wouldn't put it past Victor to have Terrace, Eric and Anthony be in this challenge. How would he do it? Victor loves me so much and want me to be happy he would try anything to resolve it. I can't let it go down like this." Angel thought deeply.

She took off her blindfold and walked slowly to the microphone staring at Victor with a smile.

"I thank everyone from the depths of my heart for making this a memorable occasion. To my brother, a special thank you. When I accepted the challenge presented, I had no idea it would be so intriguing. Being blindfolded, I could understand; but distorting the voices was an act of a genius."

Every one began to laugh.

"To each distorted voice I heard, the appropriate Bible verses were quoted. Honestly, if I could choose you all, I would."

"But you can't my love," Victor loudly shouted in fun. "What number did you select? Let's not keep the gentleman in suspense any longer."

"My brother is right," Angel sighed. "However, easier said than done. Victor, I realize your intentions were honest. It took me some time to really understand the challenge. It would not be just or honest for me to choose this way because each person involved deserves so much more. The voices were distorted but I knew who the person was just by listening to the Bible verse they recited. I refuse to diminish what we shared this way. The scripture verses that pierced my heart came from one, three and five. Twenty-five thousand dollars will still be given to the charity or institution in the name of challengers two and four. Thank you all."

Victor, Terrance, Eric and Anthony stared at each other in shock. Everyone else looked at each other trying to wonder what just happened. Victor, amazed at Angel's deductions, thanked the people who were there and gave them permission to leave. As each left, a personal gift was given. In the midst of Angel preparing to leave Eric, Anthony and Terrance approached her. Each had a different bouquet of beautiful flowers. An array of the flowers she loved, Tulips, Rose Flower, and Flowers of Paradise. Angel began to cry.

"I'm sorry for the conflict I've caused in each of your lives. It truly was unintentional. I was selfish. Terrance, Eric, I wanted to enjoy what each of you brought into my life without taking into consideration the harm and mistrust it caused you. Anthony, you were truly the innocent one who saved me from myself. I did to you what men have been doing to women for centuries...."

Angel was interrupted.

"Angel, this is not the time or place. I speak for all of us when I say you are a beautiful and talented young lady and we all love you. Let's end this now, you go home with your brother and promise to call us next week," Anthony said to Angel with the consent of Terrance and Eric.

"Ok, I am exhausted both physically and mentally. I will talk with each of you next week." Angel looked at Victor and said, "Let's go home."

Terrance, Eric and Anthony kissed Angel and quietly walked away. Victor placed his arms around his sister's waist and escorted her to his car.

Angel got home, said goodnight to her brother then proceeded to her bedroom. She turned on the Jacuzzi waves in the bath tub to take a long, hot soaking bath. While in such a relaxing mood, her mind began to revisit the past several hours. The three men who had issues with each other regarding her, in one room, together, supporting her. She promised to contact each of them next week. How is she going to handle it?

Divine intervention was summoned. Time passed very quickly, Angel honored her promise. She decided to do it in the order the conflict started.

"Good morning Eric, how are you?" Angel asked in a sweet voice.

"Good morning my beloved Angel. I am GREAT now that I have you on the telephone. How can I help you today?" Eric responded.

"Can we meet today?"

"Yes, I'm on my way?" Eric said in excitement.

Angel laughing, "Eric, I didn't say where."

"I know, I just assumed your house. Sorry, where my love?"

"I'd really like to meet at your place."

"No problem, I'll pick you up and bring you back to my place. Too late to say you had planned to drive I'm already in my car driving."

"You are too much," Angel said laughing. "I'll be waiting. Drive safely."

Eric arrived at Angel's house. He jumped out of his car and just as he was about to knock, the door opened. Angel and Eric, for several long minutes, shared the sweetest embrace.

"Since no one is here, it doesn't make since to have you drive back to your place. Come in and let's talk." Angel escorted Eric to the living room.

"Angel, yesterday is gone. It's impossible to change the past. I want to leave the past in the past and start fresh from today. I already know the direction I would like our relationship to go. I just need to know what it is you want. I pray it includes me, if not, as shard as it would be, I would be the best friend you will ever have."

Angel looked at Eric with great admiration. "You have just taken a load off my mind and heart. I had no idea what to say to you or how to say it. Thank you Eric. You know I promised to speak with not only you but Terrance and Anthony also. I decided to call you first. Now, I must speak with the others. Would it be acceptable to you if I talked to them?"

"Sure my love. I want no doubts in your mind or heart. I've got all the time in the world."

Eric got up, held Angel again and left. Several minutes elapsed, Angel grabbed her purse then drove to Mario's for coffee. While sipping on her coffee, and to her surprise, in walked Terrance who immediately saw her.

*Complicated Love*

Without any hesitation, Terrance approached the table where Angel was sitting alone.

"My blessed and favored day," Terrance said. "May I please join you?"

"Incredible," Angel looked up and said to Terrance. "Yes, please do. I'm surprised to see you here at this time of the day? No work today?"

"Fortunately, yes. I couldn't get you out of my mind. Seeing and being with you at your graduation opened my heart to the empty feelings I've tried to mask away. The only place I could think of to reconnect with you, unfortunately for me, was this diner. I had no idea you would be here."

Angel gave Terrance a perplexed look. "You think fate intervened?"

"I call it divine intervention," Terrance exclaimed reaching across the table to hold Angel's hand. "I came back here to punish myself for the behavior I rudely exhibited toward you. Please, please forgive me. Can you find it in your heart to bury that in the past? Can we just start over again?" At this point Terrance's voice was trembling.

"Terrance you can be assured from this point on I will never lie to you again. With that being said, I met Eric earlier, we talked briefly. I had planned to meet him, instead he came to my house, we discussed our lives and ironically he said the same thing you just said, whatever happened in the past will stay in the past."

"So where to from here? I feel it's too soon for a definite decision on your part. Thank you for telling me about your meeting with Eric. However, there is one more person you have to talk with, Anthony. I'm in a better place mentally now because I know WHAT GOD HAS FOR ME, I WILL GET. If your decision results with me being a dear friend, I won't like it, but I can live with it. The only thing I ask is that you don't cut me completely out of your life." With that being said, Terrance got up, kissed Angel then proceeded to walk away.

Angel sat a little longer sipping on her coffee. She began to think, some women can't get one good, devoted man. So far today, I have two. God help me and let your will for my life be done, not mine. She paid her bill and left the diner to go home. In the midst of her driving home she decided to visit Anthony.

"Let me talk to Anthony so that complete healing and direction can be per sued."

When Angel parked in front of Anthony's home, she picked up to cell to call him.

"What a pleasant surprise, Angel. How are you?" Anthony said in a relaxing voice.

"I'm fine, are you busy?" Angel asked.

"If I was, I'm not now and will never be too busy to stop whatever I'm doing to speak with you. Where are you?" Anthony asked.

"Don't be alarmed or upset, I'm sitting in my car in your driveway."

Angel heard the cell drop.

"Oh my goodness, he's angry. Let me leave before I make matters worse."

Before she could start the engine of her car Anthony was reaching for her door handle.

"Open the door baby, open the door," Anthony screamed as he stood at her car door with no shoes on his feet.

"I thought I had upset you for showing up without an invitation," Angel said as she unlocked her door."

"Upset me, honey first of all you could never upset me. I was sitting looking at the pictures I took at your graduation praying that you would call. Girl you have just made my day."

Anthony quickly opened the car door, picked Angel up and carried her into his home. Once in the house he buried his head into her chest and began to weep. Angel, holding him, also began to weep.

"Anthony, stop! There's no need for you to be acting this way." Angel said wiping her eyes and his.

"Get up, I'll make us some hot tea."

Anthony did as he was told to do and followed Angel into his kitchen.

"I am so happy that you decided to drive to see me. I wanted to call you but I couldn't take the chance of you feeling as if I was pressuring you into a decision. Thanks for the surprise. I am so elated to have you here, let's talk about you, nothing and no one else unless you choose to do so."

Angel had composed herself. She looked at Anthony and began to sing:

> "You came into my life so suddenly. You never put any claims on me. You put aside your broken heart from your previous relationship, to console me, a stranger you met in the street."

"Your voice is as sweet as your name, an angelic voice whose name is Angel." Anthony took the tea cups from Angel then proceeded to follow her into the living room.

"Anthony," Angel said as she looked at him. "It became perfectly clear to me what I have to do."

"Regarding?" Anthony replied.

*Complicated Love*

"The situation I've created with you, Terrance and Eric."

After that response from Angel, she kissed Anthony and left. He was astonished as well as perplexed. He didn't attempt to stop her. He looked at her leaving and mumbled, "I will always love you no matter what you decide to do."

Angel knew exactly what she had to do in order to set free Eric, Terrance, Anthony and herself.

This had to be done prior to her trip to Paris. Angel arrived at her house and immediately set her plan into motion. She texted all involved with the following text:

> It is imperative that we meet tomorrow at 8:00pm at the Hilton on Rockaway Beach. If I don't see you there, I'll Understand. No responses please, just be there.
>
> Love,
> Angel

Eric, Terrance and Anthony received the text message. In their minds they knew Angel was about to make her decision. They were absolutely correct.

The next morning Angel got up, said her prayers asking for the right words to say. She also prayed for peace and understanding to be present. She decided to get to the Hilton much earlier to locate where the conversation would be held. It was a beautiful day and the forecast predicted a beautiful sunset. Perfect, she thought. I will reserve seats so that our conversation will be held watching the sunset over the blue ocean.

Angel got to the hotel and awaited her guest. The three men arrived simultaneously. Angel greeted them and escorted them to the beach. The sun was beginning to set over the waters.

"I invited you all here, together, to inform you of the hardest decision I've ever had to make. I've prayed, I've cried and for all involved, here's the choice I've made."

She looked directly into the eyes of her lovers.

"You all have expressed the desire to remain in my life and for that, I am so grateful. I chose to meet here because with the smell of ocean intertwined with the beauty of the sunset, it all helped in reinforcing my ability to summon up the strength for this meeting. I want you to know without a shadow of a doubt, I love you all in your distinctive ways. The burden of truth lies solely with me because I was the one who deceived you. It was unintentional, but the fact is, I, Angel, was the guilty one. I pray that our lives will always share future precious moments. It was from you all that I was told to let go of the past. So with that mindset, we must proceed into the future with utmost respect and love. I will be leaving to go to Paris next week. There is no other decision except to let you know for now, YOU ALL ARE FREE. I hope that we stay in touch as friends." Angel walked over, kissed each one, and then walked away.

*Complicated Love*

Eric, Terrance and Anthony starred at each other in shock and dismay. Silently each one walked off the beach. The beautiful sunset no longer appeared beautiful.

"It will not end this way," Anthony thought to himself.

"You will be mine," Eric thought.

Terrance weeping, "Lord, what can I do?"

By the time Angel reached her home she was in a total disarray. Sobbing, heavily, she jumped out of her, leaving car door open, She ran inside of her home, ran upstairs, and jumped into the shower. Immediately after her shower, she grabbed a towel and fell on her bed, on her stomach, still uncontrollably crying. Fortunate for her, she unknowingly and unsuspectedly was followed.

Anthony got out of his car, noticed Angel's car door opened. He looked to make sure she was not in the car then proceeded to her front door. To his astonishment, the door was open. His mind began to play tricks with his thinking. He rushed into Angel's home and locked the front door. In fear that foul play was in the process, he did not call out her name. He frantically checked all the rooms downstairs. Everything appearing to be safe, he rushed upstairs. Angel's bedroom was located at the top of the staircase. What Anthony saw scared him. Angel was lying on her bed, barely covered with her bath towel, crying. It reminded him of how they first met. In a distant he heard the shower water still on. Anthony turned off the shower.

He didn't want to startled her so before getting into bed with her, he decided to speak.

"Angel, don't be alarmed it's me, Anthony," he said positioning his body on the bed with Angel.

Angel quickly turned over. There was Anthony, again, acting as her knight in a shining armor.

Still crying she mumbled, "Why are you here?"

"I refused to let things end the way you contorted it to end." Anthony said holding Angel lovingly. "I took the chance to come to see if I could get you to think differently. Thank God I did. You were so distraught that when you got home you not only left your car door open, you also left the front door of your house open. Thinking the worse, I secured downstairs and ran to make sure you were all right. I saw you sobbing, heard the shower still on so I turned off the shower and now I'm lying here caressing you."

"Anthony, Anthony," Angel's tears beginning to cease. "Once again I owe you, thank you from the depths of my soul."

No other words were spoken. Anthony held Angel until she fell asleep.

# NOTE FROM THE AUTHOR

As in life, all good things must come to an end. The most important thing to remember is that Jesus knew all of us before we were conceived in our mother's womb. He knew every sin we would commit and for that reason alone, He chose to die on the cross which showed His unconditional love for mankind. There's nothing we can do that Jesus has not prepared a way out for us. Don't let the enemy convince you that you are a NOBODY AND THAT GOD DOESN'T LOVE YOU. If you begin to doubt that, read John 3:16 FOR GOD SO LOVED THE WORLD HE GAVE HIS ONLY BEGOTTEN SON THAT WHOSOEVER BELIEVETH IN HIM SHALL NOT PERISH BUT HAVE EVERLASTING LIFE. Jesus will never leave you. You may walk away from Him, but He will wait patiently as you find your way back to Him. Train up a child in the way he should go and when he is old he will never depart from it. (Proverbs 22:6)

Romans 10:09-10, 13 states that if thou shalt confess with thy mouth the Lord Jesus, and shalt believe in thine heart that God hath raised him from the dead, THOU SHALT BE SAVED. For with the heart man believeth unto righteousness; and with the mouth confession is made unto salvation for whosoever shall call upon the name of the Lord, SHALL BE SAVED.

With an earnest and sincere heart, say the Sinner's Prayer. Believe what you say, claim it and begin to walk in victory. You have been saved and your name will be written in the LAMB'S BOOK OF LIFE.

**HEAVENLY FATHER, I COME TO YOU ASKING FORGIVENESS OF MY SINS. I CONFESS WITH MY MOUTH AND BELIEVE WITH MY HEART THAT JESUS IS YOUR SON, AND THAT HE DIED ON THE CROSS THAT I MAY BE FORGIVEN AND HAVE ETERNAL LIFE IN HEAVEN. I BELIEVE THAT JESUS ROSE FROM THE DEAD AND I ASK YOU RIGHT NOW TO COME INTO MY LIFE AND BE MY PERSONAL LORD AND SAVIOUS. I REPENT OF MY SINS AND WILL WORSHIP YOU ALL THE DAYS OF MY LIFE. I CONFESS WITH MY MOUTH THAT I AM BORN AGAIN AND CLEANSED BY THE BLOOD OF JESUS, IN JESUS NAME. AMEN**

God is very forgiving. Give Him your life and live. The heaven rejoices whenever the lost finds their way home, TO JESUS CHRIST.